To Daniel,
Thanks for all of your invaluable advice,
encouragement and support. And most of all,
thank you for your friendship!

1

White. It was the color that surrounded and suffocated her for 23 hours each day. The one-hour temporary reprieve which permitted her to walk around a thirty by thirty square, concrete slab did little to ease her anxiety and loneliness. If anything, it enhanced those feelings and made her feel as if she was a hamster trapped in a cage. Leg shackles, combined with handcuffs through a waist chain, severely restricted her movement. There were two phones installed on the wall to the right of the door that opened into the rec yard, but wouldn't benefit her due to the limitations placed upon her by the judge. The volleyball net that was used by the females in general population was taken down prior to her scheduled rec time, which only fueled her hatred of this place.

Her first week at the prison had been eye-opening,

frightening, and painful for the officers who were assigned to her rotation. Deputy Rogers was given a broken nose, two fractured ribs and part of her cheek was bitten off from her first encounter with Elena. Severe restrictions had been placed on any and all movement, and interactions concerning her. Even her meals were served to her in confinement, through the metal food flap in her cell door. The first three days she'd been allowed to eat in the chow hall, at a table by herself and apart from the other inmates, but at least she'd been in sight and sound of them. God, how she missed other people. Not the people themselves, but the game, manipulation, and mutilation she employed when dealing with them.

She hated to think of how long she would be forced to endure this hell. The silence was deafening and combined with the isolation from the other unfortunate souls that inhabited the prison, she wondered how she had managed to not kill someone during her incarceration.

Not to mention the effect on her already unstable mental state. Did having full length conversations with oneself point the arrows towards the end destination of insanity? Possibly. The concrete cell she now called home was dull, to say the least. A metal toilet, sink, green smock, old ratty blanket, and mattress were what occupied her cell. Due to the nature of her crimes and her homicidal, violent tendencies, all other amenities were forfeited. The first few nights had found her curled up on the flat mattress, in the fetal position, as tears rolled down her face. Not remorse for the things she'd done, just a frustration and sadness by how everything had turned out.

How had it gotten so fucked up?

The answer was clear enough, but she shied away from it, not giving the mocking voice in her head the satisfaction.

The night Gabe had brought in that younger musician, Dylan, was the catalyst that brought about her family's downfall. Tears threatened to come as she thought about the events of that day. Things had turned ugly and bloody.

Footsteps echoed outside her cell brought her mind back to the present. By the sound of their footfalls, she knew who was here to see her again. It wasn't chow time so she knew someone had come to see her. Visitors were a privilege she was not allowed, but the no visitors rule was a joke with her. Friends were a luxury she'd never had anyway. These men arriving at the facility weren't just some random people from the street. It was the two detectives from the previous afternoon. The information they'd had at their disposal was sketchy, mostly theoretical, full of holes, and lacked vital information that only she could give. The statements of the officers on scene were taken at face value due to all the shock and confusion. The number of victims they'd originally reported was fourteen.

If only that was the case.

It was upwards of thirty-five that she could recall. The faces of all of them manifested behind her closed eyes on a regular basis but failed to bring about any feelings of guilt. If anything, reliving those moments helped pass the time and gave her a sense of satisfaction and pleasure.

She hopped to her feet as the lock on the food flap disengaged with a clank. It wouldn't do good to appear weak or beaten down in front of them. She was damned if she was going to let them see that this depressing, white hell got under her skin like a festering splinter.

"Let's go Rifflet. Your friends are here to see you again," the female deputy said, holding a pair of handcuffs in her hands.

3

With a smile she sniffed once, not willing to give Sanchez the satisfaction of the response she so clearly craved. The other officer was a male, T. Roberts according to his vest, and kept both hands placed in front of him, and his eyes were daggers directed in her direction. A few days prior she'd given him quite the kick to his most sensitive area and he was not going to make the same mistake again. The beating she'd received was worth the look of pain plastered on his face.

Time to have a bit more fun. Elena felt the first handcuff go on and started tensing, knowing what response she would elicit. Sanchez tried pulling her other hand closer and Elena refused to budge.

"You're going to have to work for it, Sanchez," she whispered menacingly.

"Roberts, come hold her hand. Bitch is pulling away from me."

Deputy Roberts walked up and took hold of the arm that was already secured in the handcuffs as Sanchez fought with Elena for control of her other arm. A light brushing on his palm caused him to cringe. Elena's fingertips were slowly caressing his inner palm.

"Jesus, hurry up Sanchez!"

"Stop pretending you don't like it. I bet you've got a hard on for me right now."

Sanchez, seeing what Elena was doing, twisted Elena's other wrist the wrong way until her body stiffened in pain, or was that pleasure? Moving her wrist into the handcuff, she kept the wrist pinned in that stressed painful position.

"Alright, you can let me go now," Elena said, trying to keep the strain out of her voice. "I'll be good, I promise."

Roberts shook his head as both deputies stood back from

the cell door. Every interaction he'd had with this inmate had been uncomfortable if not painful.

"Sanchez to Controls, open cell 6," Sanchez stepped back as the door clicked and opened slowly.

With a wink, she blew Roberts a kiss as she walked past. It made her happy to see his jaw clench in anger. It wasn't hard to see that he was turned on by her the first time he'd laid eyes on her. He was in his early twenties, and she'd seen his eyes rove over her on prior occasions. The things she would do to him if she were given the chance.

"You and I could have some real fun together. A bloody good time."

2

The dripping had lessened considerably during the last twenty minutes. Shuffling and voices from the other side of the door could be vaguely heard, but inside the storeroom only the occasional drop on the floor disturbed the eerie silence. Most of the room was blanketed in darkness. Had there been windows, the sun would have provided some illumination of the carnage. The light seeping in from underneath the door was weak and barely penetrated the dark. It had taken a few minutes for her eyes to adjust to the dark of the room.

Another drop fell on the already slick floor.

Lying on her back, Elena looked upwards into the lifeless eyes that stared back. Lifting her hand, she touched the pale, cold skin of his face and smiled warmly. The memory of watching the light leave his eyes and his soul pass on to whatever awaited in the afterlife was one she would not forget. Her face was the last thing he'd seen before departing this world and that was something she didn't take lightly. It was the closest thing to witnessing something supernatural or otherworldly she would ever experience.

"Don't look so down. We had our fun didn't we handsome?"

Shifting slightly on her back produced strange, squelching sounds. The bottom of her cream-colored shirt and ripped blue jeans were soaked through. There would be no salvaging them at this point. Another drop fell next to her face adding to the steadily growing pool of blood that she was lying in.

The drain underneath the chair did wonders for keeping the floor empty of fluid buildup but not when it was intentionally blocked. A blood stained, black shirt covered it, shoved into the holes to keep the drain from working properly. Elena tilted her head to the side so that she would be able to catch the next fat drop of blood on her tongue. It landed with a plop sending shivers of delight coursing through her body.

* * *

Sitting on the counter in the kitchen, Gabe gnawed lazily at a carrot while occasionally stirring the pot that was steaming next to him. The things he did erased any hopes for him to have a taste for meat. Maybe he would go Vegan in the future.

His mother had just finished the last of the pies for the day and was washing her hands. She was an obsessive hand washer. He could recall several times where she'd washed her hands to the point of bleeding raw. He'd heard on one of the episodes of Dr. Phil that stress could do that to a person. A clanking from outside and the sound of the hose meant that Jameson was washing his tools. Expecting perfection, he didn't trust anyone else to clean his tools. A firm believer that if one wanted something done right, one must do it themselves. Bleach and other cleaning supplies cluttered one of the shelves behind the work bench. He would take his time as he stripped his tools of all traces of anything human.

"Would you mind taking these pies to the fridge to cool down?" Eleanor asked, motioning to the four finished pies next to her. Two pecan, one apple, and one peach cobbler.

Hopping down, Gabe took one in each hand, balancing the other two on each arm, and headed to the storeroom. They needed a couple of hours to get to the right temperature before being served to the customers. Being careful to not drop the pies, he approached the door, rear first, opening the door with his back, and nearly dropped the pies at the disturbing sight in front of him.

Elena was kneeling in a pool of blood, making out with the dead body. He almost gagged as the kiss continued for longer than necessary. He knew his sister was teetering on the edge of full blown psychotic and trying to deny it wasn't working anymore.

Gabe deposited the pies on the rack next to him and rushed over to his sister. He yanked her to her feet, separating her from the corpse.

"What the fuck are you doing?"

The hose was still running which was a good sign. Gabe was the only one who knew how sick and twisted his sister was. If Jameson knew that Elena harbored certain tendencies and desires... he would blow his top.

"You know what dad would do if he walked in here and saw this? You've got to be more careful sis. What were you thinking?"

She smiled innocently and shrugged her shoulders as blood dripped down from her hair, face, and shirt.

"Go clean yourself up before dad comes in."

Without a word, she hurried out of the room, avoiding the kitchen and her mother, as she crept her way to her room. Picking up the pies, Gabe put them in the fridge like he'd originally intended before intruding on his sister's perverted fantasy. He looked at the clock above the worktable. Just under two hours until the first customers started showing up.

With a disgusted grunt, he bent down and yanked the bloodied shirt from the drain, allowing the blood to escape. His sister was seriously fucked up, but he considered it his job to protect her, from herself and their father. Gabe couldn't ignore the fact that Elena was getting progressively worse. He tossed the ruined shirt into the corner, leaving it to deal with later.

There was no question that the man in front of him was no longer in the realm of the living. He pushed the man's head back, cold and clammy, as he took out his knife to cut the ropes from his legs and arms. Gabe didn't want the body to fall into him. He would need to work in a timely fashion to get this next part done.

The part of the process that he dreaded most and had never gotten used to.

The hack saw sat in its normal resting place on his father's worktable, next to the box of black trash bags. This was the one tool that Jameson allowed Gabe to use in order to perform the task that he had no desire to do himself. So, he delegated it to his son. Quick, shallow breaths through his mouth was the key to keeping himself from vomiting as he started cutting above the knee.

3

Hand under the soft, gray pillow his head rested on, body nestled under the thick blankets of the king size bed his wife had just purchased from Mattress World, he was tucked safely away from the rigors of the world. Sprinklers running outside created a nice white noise to fall asleep to. A sneeze from his right rudely interrupted his much-needed cat nap and his eyes popped open as a few droplets landed on his right arm.

"Bless you."

"Thanks," Mac responded, wrinkling his nose.

Instead of basking in the quiet, comfort of his bedroom, Warren was sitting in a restaurant parking lot with his partner in their cruiser. A twinge in the left side of his neck showed it had been a bit longer than a simple half hour nap.

Still no word on the missing young man which was

more than frustrating. Before moving forward on the next leg of this day, he needed to eat and build up his energy. Working a double required more than the routine boost. Two cups of coffee and a decent meal would go a long way towards replenishing him and granting him a second wind.

"I'm gonna go in there and see if they can whip us up something quick and easy. I know you're exhausted and haven't been getting much sleep lately. Why don't you just get a bit more sleep?"

Warren sighed and pointed to the sign on the door. 'We Open at 10:00'. He was starting to regret throwing out the stale breakfast sandwich. It would have been better than nothing. His stomach growled in agreement.

"That's just for civilians. You know they've got to have things started in the kitchen by now. I'll just go in, be my charming self, and see what I can do."

Warren motioned extravagantly towards the entrance of the establishment. "Be my guest good sir, but don't bother with a smile. It won't do you much good."

Mac scoffed at him as he exited the car. Hitching up his pants, he strode to the door at a determined pace. Warren informed Dispatch of their current location. Maneuvering himself into a more comfortable position to avoid any more tension in his neck, he shut his eyes for a bit, hoping to give his mind a break.

Falling asleep had always come easily to him. Working nights and having a tight, busy schedule during the day nurtured the mindset of sleeping whenever the hell you get the chance. Within moments his mind was drifting off into dream land.

* * *

February 17th, 1985

It took time to develop nerves of steel and he just didn't have them yet. Being his third week on the job, no one would expect it of him either. He was with his field training officer, and they were responding to a domestic disturbance call. Not knowing what to expect, he just followed procedure and whatever his FTO instructed him to do concerning the call. In his mind, Warren was envisioning the typical abuse scenario.

Husband beats wife on a regular basis. Neighbors call to report the incident when it gets too loud, blah blah blah. How wrong he was.

As they pulled into the apartment complex, Warren expected to hear screaming, things being broken, and a crying woman standing in the midst of it all trying to weather the storm. No whirlwind of craziness greeted them. It was quiet when they approached the apartments, with only five of the twelve spaces occupied. Reflecting on it later, the stillness is what initially set his nerves on edge. The complex wasn't large by any means, two stories with six apartments on the first floor and six on the second floor, so they wasted no time and started searching for the apartment numbers. It was a shabby place, with black mold on the walls, and lawn maintenance was clearly not high on the priority list.

Second floor. Apartment number 203. The complex was nothing to write home about from the outside and once they entered the stairwell to head upstairs, it was abundantly clear that the inside was no different. Peeling, yellow walls hid under the light coating of dirt and dust. Faded, reddish brown carpets with numerous stains of God knew what stretched down the hallway. It was apparent that the owners were not big on upkeep or maintenance of any kind. No tenants were in the hallway, and they didn't hear any yelling, or anything that would point towards a domestic disturbance call.

"You sure this is the right building?" Warren whispered.

His training officer nodded and raised a finger to his lips, trying to listen for any clue as to what was going on behind the door. Nothing. He nodded to Warren again and gave two knocks on the door that had the 203 hanging crooked above it.

Silence. Two more knocks and a stern order. "Police. Open the door!"

A stirring on the other side, followed by light footsteps to the door. Warren moved from one foot to the other, trying to keep still but failing to do so as the adrenaline started coursing through his veins. The door opened to a point, stopped by the chain, giving a glimpse of a woman in her early thirties. Her eyes didn't seem to give any indication of fear or worry that one would expect, and her clothes didn't seem disheveled.

"How can I help you officers?"

His training officer spoke with a clear, unclipped tone. "Good morning ma'am. I'm Officer McDaniels and this is Officer Warren. We received a few noise complaints regarding this apartment. Is everything okay?"

Warren cleared his throat and moved slightly, getting a better view into the apartment. She filled in the gap well, closing off any hope of seeing past her. Alternating glances between both of them, she smiled and asked for one moment. The door shut and the chain was removed.

"You're welcome to come in. My husband is… indisposed currently, but I can answer any questions you have."

They followed her into the apartment, and she took a seat in a weathered, torn recliner that had seen better years.

Nothing seemed out of the ordinary. Warren's initial thought was that it had been a prank call by an annoying neighbor. No noticeable bruises, or cuts on her person. What was going on?

Both were making observations and taking mental photographs of the apartment. The only thing out of the ordinary was the bulging, blue, travel suitcase that sat crooked against the couch.

"Can I get you gentlemen something to drink?"

"Tea if you have it, thank you."

With a nod, she left the room and went into what Warren presumed was the kitchen area. He knew the tea request was just to give them some time to look around. With a gesture from McDaniels, Warren performed a quick search of the room and hallway leading out of it as the woman busied herself in the kitchen. No sign of the husband in the hallway or bathroom. Where was he?

Warren swore under his breath as his foot connected painfully with the suitcase and it didn't budge.

It was damn heavy!

"What the fuck is in this?" he whispered.

His training officer shrugged as he approached but froze halfway to Warren. In one smooth motion, he undid the clip on his sidearm. Warren's confusion vacated him as his view shifted to the briefcase and to the side of it that was nestled up to the couch. Blood was dribbling out of it in streams, staining the carpet and spreading fast.

The sound of the refrigerator door closing brought him back to his senses and he had his gun drawn as well. McDaniels approached the kitchen and shouted at her to get down on the floor, hands behind her head, etc. She followed the orders without question or resistance of any kind as the handcuffs were placed on her.

Dropping to his knees, Warren shifted the suitcase carefully and opened the latches. Warren would be forever haunted by the contents for the rest of his life and wish he hadn't been the one to open it. The woman had gotten fed up with her husband's laziness, drugged him, and then proceeded to cut him into small enough pieces to be fit into their traveling suitcase. Holding down the bile that was creeping up his throat was a challenge, but he managed. The body parts, arranged in an organized manner of sorts, caused a cold sweat to break out over his skin.

It was obvious that she'd had a breakdown of some kind. She never should have allowed them entry into her apartment or at least moved the evidence prior to opening the door, if she'd wanted to get away with the crime.

* * *

Warren's eyelids fluttered as the nightmare culminated in his opening of the dreaded, blue suitcase for what must have been the hundredth time over the past two years. Recurring nightmares were common for him. Alcohol helped to dampen these and permit him some nights without any dreams. Even when he realized it was a dream, he remained powerless against changing the outcome. Just one time, he'd like to not open the damned suitcase.

4

Knocking on the door for the third time, Mac was ready to head back to the car and break the bad news to Warren. If they wanted to satisfy their appetites, shitty gas station food seemed to be their only option. There was no window on the door and the ones to the side were near impossible to see through due to the reflecting sun and the thin coating of dust and dirt. He could hear light footsteps approach from the other side and hope burned bright again for a decent meal.

A lock turned and an attractive older woman opened the door. Surprise showed briefly on her face but quickly vanished as she fell into her role as hostess.

"Can I help you Officer?"

She seemed to be in her early fifties. Dark hair speckled with gray fell to just past her shoulders, fair skin... the stained cooking apron around her middle was the only thing not complimenting her appearance and figure. Eyebrows raised, she leaned toward him waiting patiently for his answer.

"Yes, sorry. My partner and I have been working the night shift and just found out that our day is getting extended. I know your sign says you don't open until ten, but is there any way you could whip something up in the kitchen for us?" Mac said with a smile, then patted his pocket. "We're good tippers."

She tilted her head to the side, seeming to consider whether to invite him in or shut the door in his smiling face. *Maybe Warren was right. I shouldn't have smiled.* Sensing the need in his voice, she nodded.

"I'm sure we can rustle up something for you two. Come on in. Will your partner be joining you?"

Stepping back from the door she extended her hand, inviting him inside. A look behind him showed Warren snoozing away, head resting against the window. If the inside of the place doesn't look like a dump and seemed worthy of Warren's standards, then he'd wake him up. No reason to disturb him now.

"He's pretty exhausted. I'll let him rest for a bit."

The inside of the restaurant wasn't impressive or extravagant. The lighting was dark and uninviting giving the whole place an ominous feel. Mac followed the woman and couldn't help but second guess his decision. Unappealing green walls, multi-colored stains permanently dried on the floor presumably from what customers dragged in on their shoes, and the unavoidable spills that occur didn't do much for boosting Mac's confidence. A few pictures and paintings adorned the walls, probably in hopes of livening the place up, but they failed miserably.

A family portrait, of the owners no doubt, sat dead center on the far wall. Seeing the face of the woman he was following standing in the picture gave that away. The only person smiling in the photo was the younger woman, who he secretly was hoping to meet. The other three had a somber look about them that made it seem like they were posing at a funeral or something equally disheartening.

On the opposite wall rested a faded photograph of a football stadium. Looked to be Joe Robbie Stadium where the Dolphins were scheduled to play their first game later this month. At a passing glance he couldn't be too sure though.

One painting caused him to stumble. A gorgeous woman laying on a lush, purple couch covered by only a red blanket. The clash of color is what first drew his eye, but the face caused his attention to linger. An uncanny resemblance to the younger woman in the portrait. What a weird thing to display in a restaurant.

The only thing that kept him from bolting for the door was the mouth-watering smells that were coming from what he assumed to be the kitchen. She motioned to a table, next to the picture of the football stadium but without a window. There was a light above the table that gave off just enough light to keep him from complaining. She placed a menu in front of him. They seemed to offer quite a few options to satisfy a diversity of appetites.

"Elena will be out shortly to take your order and can answer any questions you may have about the menu. Enjoy your meal," she said with a small smile and nod of her head.

5

If he had a hand free, Gabe would have slapped himself for his stupidity in assuming he could carry all three bags at one time and get through the door smoothly. It was an issue of size not strength. Two bags were gripped tightly in his left hand, fingers digging into the plastic, and the heavier bag in his left. The contents of each bag were of differing size and weight which complicated any movements he made. Turning sideways, he wiggled his way through the doorway, but the larger bag got hung up on the edge of the door, stretched, and then began to tear.

In frustration, he kicked the door shut. Hard. Droplets of blood now marked his passage.

Trudging across the dirt, sweat dripped down his forehead. Gabe dropped the bags into the open bed of his truck. A few seconds went by, and blood started to collect in the bottom of the truck. He could see a hand sticking out of the side of the larger bag through the opening caused by the door.

"Fuck it," he muttered, shutting the bed of the truck.

Rinsing out the truck was something he would worry about when he returned from the dump site. His mind kept replaying the events of the night before. The confrontation with his father had been a breakthrough for him on a massive scale. Fights between them had always been one-sided with Gabe on the losing side taking the brunt of his father's barrage of punches and kicks. Last night, while nursing his bloody nose, he made a vow to himself. He was through taking shit from his father. If things continued to escalate, Jameson was going to find out just how far his son was willing to take things. The truth of the revelation Gabe was experiencing was freeing and frightening at the same time.

Gabe was prepared to wrench himself free of his father's control, violently if necessary. The days of him blindly following his father's orders and instructions were behind him. A new day was dawning in his mind, and he would make sure it was one that Jameson would never forget.

6

A loud bang yanked Warren out of his recurring nightmare. Where had it come from? Yawning, he rolled down the window for some fresh air.

Scanning the area in front of him presented him a scene of a young man toting three trash bags out of what looked to be a back room of some sorts.

Based on the layout of the building, it was connected to the restaurant in some fashion. The sides of the room were rusted near the bottom, and weeds were beginning to crawl up the sides. No windows that he could see. Probably just a storeroom for supplies.

The agitation on the man's face was enough for Warren to piece together that it was the man slamming the door that had awoken him. Nothing out of the ordinary. Just another disgruntled employee that hated his job and was picturing his boss's head being between the door and the jamb when he'd shut it.

He almost resumed his nap when he noticed something odd. Squinting his eyes, he bolted upright in his seat once his mind registered what his eyes were transmitting. Sleep was long forgotten when he realized it was a bloody human hand protruding from a hole in the bag. His instincts kicked into high gear.

Warren grabbed for the radio to inform dispatch of what was taking place in front of him. He'd just depressed the button when he spotted movement to his left.

A shadow.

He'd never even heard the person approaching. The butt of a shotgun connected with his face and then blackness.

* * *

Jameson yanked open the door in a fit of unholy rage. He hit the man again in the side of the head with the shotgun to ensure that he was out. His limp body fell out of the car into the dirt. How stupid could his son be? He was going to ruin everything he had worked so hard to build. If he wasn't careful, it could all come crashing down around him. Things had just gotten a bit sticky. The officer looked to weigh a bit over two hundred pounds, but Jameson would have no trouble in getting him to the storeroom. The real issues were the partner inside, disposing of the vehicle, and the voice that was coming through the radio asking for the officer to say again. Flexing his fingers, he rested the shotgun against the side of the car and put things into motion.

Hesitating when action was required could be disastrous. He remembered how his own father beat the knowledge into him and had learned from that experience. Take the curve balls life throws at you and keep moving. Jameson gritted his teeth and adjusted his grip on the unconscious man.

7

Gabe fell to the ground in a heap under the blows his father continued to rain down up on him. Curling himself into a ball does little in the ways of protection and only succeeded in angering Jameson even further. All thoughts of bettering his father and becoming his own man evaporated under the ferocity of the attack. Blood fell from a cut above his eye and Gabe pulled his knees tighter towards his chest to give Jameson fewer sensitive areas to hit. So much for being brave and standing up to his asshole of a father. *The bastard sucker-punched me. I didn't even see it coming.*

How was it his fault that the fucking cops had shown up? He'd done everything asked of him. Whose brilliant idea was it to use people as a meat supply in the first place? It sure as hell wasn't Gabe's. The mastermind behind this whole operation was Jameson.

A cry of anger and sadness from the direction of the storage room. Though his vision was blurred by blood, he could see his mother rushing towards him. A deep breath of gratitude and relief. The beating had stopped, temporarily if he had to guess.

Eleanor managed to push her husband back and away from her son. Mainly because she had surprised him. First mistake.

Her concern was for her son who was a bleeding mess on the ground. Blood marred his face, and his clothes were disheveled, torn and stained. Kneeling in the soil, she whispered something to him that Jameson couldn't hear to which Gabe only nodded in reply. The widening of Gabe's eyes was the only warning she had.

Ignoring Jameson was her second mistake.

Her head was yanked back forcefully by her hair, some tearing free of the roots. Her neck screamed in protest as her muscles spasmed.

"What's running through your head woman? You think you can undermine my authority! I thought I'd gotten rid of that rebellious streak of yours." His eyes were wide and filled with a burning anger. "I guess some lessons need to be revisited."

On the last word, the back of his hand connected with her cheek and sent her sprawling upon the ground. Jameson wasn't through yet. His adrenaline was pumping. There was no denying that he got off on showing the power he had over his family.

"It's been quite some time since you've needed some correction, hasn't it? I'm more than willing to re-educate you."

Wiping the sweat from his forehead, Jameson hitched up his unkempt jeans and brought his leg back for a swift kick to her abdomen. He wanted her to cry out in pain and beg for mercy. His brow knotted in confusion as he found himself lifted into the air.

* * *

Being thought of as the helpless victim has its advantages. You tend to get lost in the background of all situations. The second Jameson had switched his focus to Eleanor, Gabe was tossed to the back-burner in his mind. Seeing his mother get knocked to the ground set off an explosion inside Gabe's mind and he allowed it to consume him.

All the rage, hate, and guilt that he'd kept locked away all those years came pouring out in a torrent and Jameson had the pleasure of receiving it. Gaining his feet, Gabe trotted toward his father. Grabbing him from behind, one hand on his belt, and one on the back of his shirt, he lifted and propelled Jameson into the side of the truck in one smooth motion. Jameson's muscles tensed but showed no other reaction as his head bounced off the side of the truck.

Jameson was in total shock. His mind was having trouble processing what was taking place. The first punch from Gabe glanced off the side of his face. The second connected with his nose, cocking it at a weird angle against his face. Two more fast jabs to his stomach. Jameson let out a grunt. If not for the truck holding him up, Jameson would have been hard pressed to remain standing. Smiling through the blood coming from his nose, Jameson wrestled for control of Gabe's arms but failed. Gabe backed off, eyes wild, and pointed in Jameson's face.

"If you ever touch her again, I will fucking kill you!" he whispered fiercely.

Breathing heavily through gritted teeth, Gabe stared his father down.

"So, you do have a pair?" Jameson said, more impressed than angry. He gingerly touched his nose and spit out a mouthful of blood. "You may be worth something after all boy."

Making himself stand up and away from the truck without flinching took a considerable measure of mental and physical strength but Jameson pulled it off. Maintaining control and dominance was crucial at this juncture. Their relationship was at a tipping point. Letting Gabe know that he was shaken up and hurt would shatter the image he'd projected. His hands trembled slightly as he forced his nose into the proper position. He closed his eyes to the pain.

Eleanor was lying on the ground, hand to her mouth. Disbelief covered her features.

"Now, clean that mess out of the bed of the truck. Then head inside. We've got to think this through and get this situation under control. And fast. All that aggression and anger will be useful in the coming hours. You've proven yourself and the timing couldn't be more perfect."

Without answering, Gabe walked over and helped his mother to her feet. Her right cheek was an angry red from the backhand and was likely to bruise at some point. Eleanor hustled inside, intentionally keeping her head forward. The door shut behind his mother and Gabe turned back to his father, still not uttering a word. He was prepared for shit to go down and a battle royale to commence.

The words that had come from his father held no meaning to Gabe. A few sentences didn't rectify a lifetime of wrongs. Taking a rag from his back pocket, Jameson wiped the blood from his nose and mouth. A smile on Jameson's face was an uncommon sight, and two in the span of a few minutes... mind-blowing. With a nod to the blood-filled truck bed, he headed back inside.

"Don't think this is through dad," he said the last word with disdain. "I meant what I said."

Something had changed. Both men knew it but neither knew how to address it any further. Gabe had switched roles from the helpless, cowardly victim to a person to be reckoned with.

8

His heart rate finally slowed to a normal rhythm as the water from the hose rinsed away the blood that had pooled in the truck bed. Sitting on the hood of the cab, he waved the hose back and forth, making sure to not leave any residue. It was sure to stain if it was given the chance to dry in the heat, not to mention the smell.

Pride swelled within him.

That was the first time he'd ever stood up to his father in such a monumental way. There had been the occasional, spontaneous remark, or curse, but nothing as significant as what had just happened. *Father... might as well call it like it is. He's nothing more than a sperm donor.*

Jameson lacked any of the qualities that would be attributed to a man worthy of the title father. Loving, encouraging, supportive, protective. All words that failed to describe Jameson, even in the slightest. For as long as Gabe could remember, Jameson had always used him as his own personal punching/kicking bag. He could stomach the harsh words and treatment if it was aimed only at him but when it came to his mother and sister…

No longer would he fulfill the role of a bystander to his father's abuse towards his mother, sister, or himself. A seed started to take root in his mind. He knew what he would have to build up the courage to do if he wanted to protect the only people he truly loved and care about. He would have to get rid of the man who'd helped bring him into this world. He was going to have to kill his own father.

Gabe cocked his head to the side as he sprayed a particularly stubborn clot in the tailgate. Shouldn't he feel sad at even the thought of doing it? Thinking of being rid of Jameson's oppressive nature brought out feelings of happiness and a sense of freedom that he'd ever only dreamt about. Yes, Gabe thought, a day of reckoning was brewing.

9

The luscious figure exiting the kitchen in front of him had his undivided attention. Any misgivings or hesitation Mac had about the strange decorations and set up of the restaurant were fast becoming memories. It had been two weeks since his last night with Kara Watkins, but it may as well have been a lifetime. As she leaned forward next to him, asking what he'd like to drink and order, he felt a stirring. The top three buttons of her light pink shirt were undone, giving him a generous glimpse, and leaving little to the imagination.

With a cough, Mac painfully shifted his gaze to her eyes and could tell she was amused, not offended in the slightest.

"Um, a coffee, no cream, two sugar."

"Sure, anything to eat handsome?"

Looking over the menu once more didn't help him in his decision. He'd barely glanced at it.

"What would you recommend? I'm not really feeling a

pull in any one direction so I'm open to trying something new."

With a smile, she leaned across him and bit down on her lower lip, pretending to scan the menu. Like she didn't know what they offered. He breathed in her scent, some type of flowery perfume, and sighed.

"I'd go with our stew as an appetizer, then perhaps the Jameson's Catch of the Day for an entree. It's one of our more popular requests."

Handing her the menu, Mac nodded. "You've sold me."

With a wink, she took the menu, brushing his hand lightly in the process. She headed back to the kitchen, making sure to sway her hips, and shot a quick glance out one of the windows she passed. Water ran off the back of the truck in little streams, as Gabe hopped down, finished with cleaning it. She knew she wouldn't have any trouble keeping the officer's attention on her and off what was happening elsewhere. Typical male behavior that was so easy to exploit, manipulate and ultimately control.

10

The calls from dispatch continued to go unanswered. Having turned off his radio, assuming that Warren would take care of anything should something come through, Mac failed to hear it. If he had, he may have wondered why Warren wasn't responding and instantly been on alert.

He did wonder why Warren hadn't come in yet but as the beautiful waitress ambled back over with his soup, he dropped that line of thinking. Probably could use the much-needed extra sleep. Who was he to interrupt that? He knew how troubled and stressful his life at home had been of late. The waitress placed the steaming bowl of soup in front of him with a smile and waited.

The anticipation on her face was a clear indication that she wanted to know his thoughts on the stew. The first bite reminded him of warm roast soaked in gravy... with a stronger flavor and different texture.

"My God," he said, stirring his spoon around, "it's

delicious! What kind of meat do you guys use? The texture is unlike anything I've ever tasted."

Elena smiled and shook her finger as he took another bite.

"It's an original family recipe. Also, we don't use anything store bought like most other restaurants do."

Both Mac and Elena jumped as a door slammed and a muffled curse came from the back of the restaurant. Elena's demeanor shifted from doting seductress to a jumpy, nervous woman. Mac fell back on what he always did in uncomfortable situations. Try and alleviate the awkwardness.

"I was going to ask you to give my compliments to your chef, but it sounds like he may be busy at the moment."

A quick shake of her head and she was back in her playful mode.

"I made the stew myself, thank you very much," she said, squeezing his shoulder gently. "I'll be back in a moment. Can I get you anything else?"

"I wouldn't say no to a diet coke," he said, scooping up another bite.

"You got it," she said with a smile.

He wasn't too worried about what was going on in the back. Nothing that concerned him. Someone probably dropped some food or something and was venting their frustration at being clumsy. With a shrug of his shoulders, he downed another spoonful of the savory stew.

11

Hefting the officer's limp body over his shoulder, Jameson made his way carefully past the restaurant, avoiding any windows. The situation was already on the verge of unraveling into a disaster. The last thing he needed was for the other cop to see his unconscious partner being carried by a stranger. He seriously doubted if he'd be able to stop the younger officer while he was busy transporting the other one. Jameson would have Elena deal with him shortly.

Taking one last glance at the road to make sure no cars were approaching, or unwanted observers passing by, he continued to the storeroom door. Opening the door wasn't an easy task but he managed. Grunting, Jameson dropped the man to the floor in a heap. At this point, he didn't care if the man hit his head or was injured even further. The countdown had already commenced on his short time left in this world.

Slamming the door shut behind him, he stalked over to

his work bench. Jameson tried to keep his anger and frustration from exploding out of him by gripping the sides of the bench tightly to the point of causing pain. He could tell that he was on the verge of a mental breakdown.

It was Gabe's fault for not taking care of the evidence properly. That little shit always found a way to dig under his skin like a festering splinter. He'd been so careful over the years to avoid the attention of the police.

He would not rot away the rest of his life behind bars!

The door opened behind him, and Elena stood in the doorway. Erring on the side of caution, she hesitated, not sure what to say, if anything. When her father was in these moods, he became unpredictable and violent. His back heaved up and down with deep breaths and she could tell he was but seconds away from losing it.

"Anything I can do to help?"

She kept her tone light and soft in hopes of reaching through his haze of anger and bringing him back to a normal state. Well... Normal for him at least.

His head lifted and after a few deeper, calming breaths Jameson recovered his composure. Elena kept still as he approached. A fake smile, one that he has perfected with time, surfaced on his face. He put his hand on her cheek, rubbing with his thumb just under her eye. His expression gave nothing in the way of what his response could be.

It took everything in her not to cringe away from his touch. The light touch could turn into a stinging slap without warning.

"Always the one to help," he responded, letting his hand drop away from her face. "I'll take care of things on this end, but do you think you can handle the one out there without too much trouble? He can't be allowed to stroll out of here and find his partner missing. I'll leave the choice of how to dispose of him to you."

A plan was already taking shape in her mind.

"I'm sure I can think of something," she said with a wink, grateful to not be the outlet for this current debacle.

12

Gabe paced back and forth in the cooling shade of the trees behind the restaurant. It was the perfect area for him to gather his thoughts and get some respite from the heat. He continued to wrestle with opposing thoughts and emotions. Part of him wanted to just slide under his father's radar and be the respectful, obedient, and willing son that Jameson clearly wanted. The other part was through with taking Jameson's shit and was ready for things to change.

Dust billowed up as he kicked at the dirt. For a split second he thought of getting in his truck and putting this shithole behind him. Never look back. Leave this horrible existence and start fresh, away from the bonds that Jameson had painfully placed upon him since childhood. A life away from the torture, dismemberment, and killing of innocent people. This wasn't the first time he'd entertained this train of thought. It was nothing more than a beautiful delusion, a false hope that he played out in his head from time to time. A tear fell from his face as he looked upon the place that he'd called home. In the window Gabe saw Elena coming out of the storeroom and he couldn't help the flood of memories that came unasked for.

* * *

Throwing the last of the necessities in the bag on top of his clothes, he went over it in his head one final time. Without proper planning, this would never work. It would blow up in his face and probably be the death of him.

Clothes, check. He had enough to last him at least a week and half. Food, check. Two cans of baked beans, three cans of creamed corn, some lunch meat, a few bags of chips. Just the bare minimum to get him started on the road. Money, check. He'd swiped sixty dollars from his father's wallet the previous night when he was passed out drunk in his reclining chair from his end of the day binge.

A sniffling from the doorway interrupted his last-minute checks. Gabe didn't have to turn around to know who he would see standing in the doorway to his room. His younger sister, Elena.

She wiped away the tears from her eyes and continued to stare at him, not saying a word. The fighting between their parents had been steadily escalating over the past few months. Screaming, fists being thrown, furniture tossed around. The restaurant business wasn't cheap and keeping it running was putting a strain on their parent's relationship. At fifteen Gabe understood enough to keep out of the way, when he could, but still managed to get beatings from his father on a weekly basis, if not every other day.

He winced as he touched the back of his head. It was scabbing over and still sore from when his father had shoved him outside, causing Gabe to fall and smash his head against the side of the truck just two days before.

Another sniff from his sister, who was just eleven, stopped his inner musings and brought home the reality of what, or rather who, he would be leaving behind. Getting out of this shit hole was one thing. Leaving his sister behind was something that hadn't even crossed his mind until now. What he'd considered to be an easy, practical decision quickly became complicated and personal.

"Come here," he whispered and motioned with his hand.

Elena entered his room and sat on the bed next to him, fresh tears coursing down her face. She was young but knew what the packed bag implied and wasn't happy with the notion that he was abandoning her. Her shoulders wracked with silent sobs. They sat on the bed together for a few minutes, Gabe's arm wrapped around her small shoulders promising her everything would be okay.

That's when the volume of their parent's voices started to increase. He felt his sister stiffen under his arm and knew without question that he couldn't leave her. She needed him and he was not going to turn his back on the one good thing in his life.

"I will never leave you."

* * *

His mother and sister's faces danced in the front of his mind, cutting his plan to ribbons. Even after seeing the monster his sister was becoming, he still couldn't walk out on her. His mother, sweet as she could be at times, was just as much a victim to Jameson's abuse as he was which left him with just one option. Everything would need to be timed perfectly for Gabe to succeed or the consequences could be deadly... for him.

13

A few wispy clouds drifted overhead across the light blue sky. A cool breeze ruffled their clothes as they arranged the blanket for their picnic. An older couple walked by, hands entwined, a young woman jogged past with her dog keeping pace by her side, and a little boy of eight years old peered intently at his red and yellow kite that was swaying in the wind above him. Warren and his wife nestled next to one another on the white and blue checkered blanket watching their son fly his kite. There was no place he'd rather be than spending his Saturday off with his wife and son. The edges of his vision started to blur and shake. What was happening? A ripple effect spread across his field of vision, and he jumped to his feet. The scenery and people melted away like dripping wax in a swirl of colors.

How did he end up here? A hospital room. There were flowers on the table next to the bed that was hidden behind the curtain encompassing the bed. Warren made his way towards the table, trying to keep his gaze from the silhouette he could just make out on the bed. Upon reading the name on the card, he shut his eyes tight, fighting the urge to cry. He was in his father's hospital room, which ended up becoming his home for his last six weeks of life. Gripping the curtain in his hand, he pulled it back revealing a shriveled, weak old man.

His father, Andrew Warren.

The scared and confused look in his eyes spoke a thousand words. He didn't recognize Warren as his son. Alzheimer's had robbed his father of his physical strength and mental prowess, turning him into a shell of his former self. The strong and intelligent man had been stripped away.

"Where is Martha? I need to talk to Martha. Or my son Scott. Where are my wife and son?"

Setting his jaw, he shattered his father's world.

"I'm Scott dad," he said in a comforting tone. "And Martha's gone. She passed away six years ago."

Watching his father break down and hearing his sobs were too much and he turned away, shutting his eyes to the burning sensation of fresh tears.

Upon opening them, Warren found the location and time frame had changed once again. A part of him understood that he was dreaming but it had all the feelings of reality. He struggled through the fog of the dream, hoping to wake up. No luck.

The bedroom was sparsely decorated. A wedding photo on the dresser, a picture of the same young couple in front of a beautiful lake, and a framed picture of the woman in graduation garb beaming, her husband next to her just as proud. The bed was made, gray sheets tucked in, pillows propped on top and white comforter folded neatly at the foot of the bed. Tidy and well-kept room if one ignored the blood.

It saturated the sheets and mattress in the center of the bed. Brain matter decorated part of the wall behind the bed. One of his first calls after his field training phase. A suicide. The wife had died of cancer and the husband couldn't deal with the pain of her loss anymore and decided to eat a bullet. Another ripple started through the room followed by a pain in his abdomen that caused him to double over. One hand on the bed he kept himself from falling to the floor. It felt like someone had taken a gut shot on him, but he was alone in the room. More pain in his chest and stomach caused him to utter a groan and fall back against the wall. Everything started to swirl in a blend of colors and fade to black.

14

Following the third kick, Warren moaned and stirred slightly, curling more into himself. His training caused him to instinctively make himself a smaller target and protect his vitals. Pain was all he knew upon waking. The room was dark, making it difficult to figure out his location, but he saw a figure standing above him.

The figure grunted as he rolled Warren over onto his back. Blood dribbled from his nose due to the stock of the shotgun becoming intimate friends with his face. Warren coughed and dragged himself into a sitting position, painfully. The man yanked his arms behind his back and secured them with Warren's own handcuffs. In one smooth motion, he hauled him to his feet.

Still groggy, Warren fought to clear his head. The man in front of him looked to be in his early to mid-fifties. Dirty white shirt, torn jeans, and medium build with a graying head of hair. Warren flexed his arms and figured he could overtake the man if given the chance. Handcuffs or no, he still could hold his own and was prepared to prove it.

Jameson stood in front of him and sneered, reading the name badge on his chest.

"You have to know that I can't let you go Officer Warren. It's very simple. I need you to listen and do so carefully."

Without warning, Warren smashed his head into Jameson's face, connecting with his left cheek. Jameson staggered back, off balance. If he hadn't turned at the last second, he would have broken his nose again. Warren's senses returned in full force along with an attitude.

"Sorry, were you saying something?"

Jameson reached tentatively for his cheek and winced. Fueled by rage and pain, Jameson tackled Warren to the floor and rained blow after blow upon his face and body. The handcuffs prevented Warren from fighting back so he used another tactic and just gave his attacker a bloody smile.

Jameson only stopped when he felt Warren's body go slack. Breathing heavily, Jameson stood up and regained his composure.

"The feisty ones always get special treatment. I've got just the thing for you."

Back in control, Jameson smiled, picked Warren up from underneath his armpits and dragged him across the room. One eye swollen shut, a piece of a tooth on the ground, and probably more damage that was unseen made him look like a fucked up human pinata. Muscles cording, Jameson got Warren up to a standing position in front of the two dangling hooks that hung from the ceiling. They were two feet in length and the curved points were always kept sharpened. Jameson lifted him up and dropped him onto the hooks.

The hooks pierced his flesh, entered through his back,

went under the collar bone, and exited at the top of his chest. The sensation of the hooks grinding against his bones was enough to bring him back from the bliss of unconsciousness.

Warren's eyes shot open.

Unintelligible sounds escaped his mouth as it opened and closed. Pain invaded his brain, and he could focus on nothing else. Jameson stood in front of him with a glint in his eyes, watching his reaction. Biting down on his lip hard enough to draw blood, Warren was determined not to give the bastard the satisfaction of hearing him scream.

He settled with grunting and blowing his breath out in rapid succession. He couldn't move an inch without waves of agony from his back, chest, and shoulders. The pressure on his collarbones was excruciating and put him mercifully on the verge of passing out. He was having little success in slowing his heart rate and breathing. The thought of killing the man standing in front of him kept him conscious and gave him something to hold onto and keep from being swept away with the tide of pain that was threatening to overtake him.

"Care to say something?" Jameson said as he placed his hand on Warren's chest and gently pushed, not bothered in the slightest by the mixture of sweat and blood he felt under his palm.

With as much venom as he could muster Warren replied in a menacing tone, "There's no getting... away with this. If I don't get to... I will take pleasure... knowing that someone else... will kill you!"

Jameson shrugged his shoulders and left the room, leaving Warren alone with his torture. A moan of pain mingled with anger escaped him after the door closed. With the blanket of darkness to comfort him, he prayed that Mac would head out to the car, see the busted out window,, call in the cavalry, and come in guns blazing.

15

He wiped his chin with a napkin upon taking his final bite of the fantastic stew and sat back in the booth, stomach pleased. If the other items on the menu were as remotely good as the stew, Warren wouldn't complain. Maybe it would even brighten his mood a bit. Thinking of Warren, his hand drifted down to his radio to turn it on and check on him. The motion stopped as Elena strolled back into the dining area from the kitchen.

Mac was prepared to order whatever she suggested; she had that kind of sway over him already. He knew his weakness and wasn't ashamed to admit it.

"The stew was incredible. You weren't kidding! Probably even better than my aunt makes back home but I'll keep that secret between you and me."

She stood next to him and laid a hand on his shoulder.

"Have you decided on what you want to order for your entree? Are you going to trust me with my suggestion?"

With difficulty, Mac directed his eyes back to the menu. He was leaning towards a burger with the works but wanted to ask her what the Jameson's Catch was because she'd suggested it earlier. From the description on the menu, it sounded damn good. A combination of steak, shrimp, and the customer's choice of fish, availability willing.

* * *

As the officer turned his attention back to the menu, Elena slid her left hand across his back so that it rested on his opposite shoulder. She was practically leaning all her weight into him. The fishing wire in her hands had gone unnoticed.

"You mentioned the Jameson's Catch earlier, what sides..."

He never finished the question. Standing up abruptly, she slipped the wire under his chin and pulled. He failed to get his hand under the wire in time and it bit deeply into his neck. The menu flew off the table along with his half-filled Diet Coke, his eyes bulged out of their sockets, and he flailed his arms trying to get a grip on Elena. The erratic movement caused blood to spray in spurts from his neck as the wire sunk deeper into his flesh. His hands scratched shallow grooves in her arms, but the table prevented him from being able to stand and get any decent leverage.

Lifting her leg and doing a little hop, she positioned herself behind him, on top of the booth, so his hands couldn't find purchase. Pushing with her legs, she pulled harder. His hand fumbled with the strap on his sidearm, but his panic kept him from getting any good grip. Within fifteen seconds the fighting stopped, and his body fell to the side.

16

Normally Eleanor kept her thoughts to herself when it pertained to what went on in the restaurant and the methods that Jameson used in acquiring the meat. But this time it was different. Things were starting to spiral out of control. Her husband had one man locked in their storeroom and another was in the dining area, not forty feet away, brutally murdered at the hands of her own daughter. And both were police officers. Her nerves were frayed.

"It's gone too far. These aren't just two random people who Gabe picked up on the side of the road. They're police officers and their disappearance will not go unnoticed like the others. All these years and not once have we had anything come back to bite us in the ass, but that's not the case here. What are you going to do with their vehicle? What happens when people come around looking for them?"

Jameson rested against the counter examining his nails, seeming to ignore her, as he picked out flecks of dirt.

"And not to mention what happened out there," she motioned to the dining area. "The atrocities you commit are one thing, but you are corrupting our children and that has to stop. Elena's becoming a monster."

Jameson lost it as the word monster left her lips. Rushing over, he closed his hand around her throat and shoved her into the wall, knocking over the utensils and rattling the bowls and plates. He leaned in close, putting his face inches away from her own.

"Don't you ever speak of my daughter that way again," he whispered in a threatening tone.

It wasn't lost on Eleanor that he referred to Elena as "my daughter" and not "ours". Fighting the tears didn't help; they fell regardless. The realization that her husband was an evil man had always lurked in her mind like a shadowy figure behind the scenes, but she'd been afraid to admit it. There was no denying it now.

Moving his hand up to her cheek, he kissed her roughly. She turned her head and pulled away, disgusted. Shaking his head, he stood back from her and headed into the dining area.

"A pathetic excuse for a wife," he muttered under his breath, just loud enough for her to hear.

Fresh tears spilled over, and she fell to the floor sobbing because of her own inability to save her family and possibly restore it. She was trapped. A sense of helplessness washed over her as she realized that a countdown had begun. The future she saw appeared dark and full of despair.

17

The thoughts boiled in his head like an overflowing kettle as he stormed out of the kitchen. He'd done everything he could to provide for his family and this was how he was repaid. An ungrateful wife, disappointing son, and...

That train of thought vanished as he entered the dining area and his anger subsided. Elena was draped across the clearly dead officer's lap. His body was propped in place against the rear of the booth and the wall, keeping him firmly in a sitting position. Hand entwined in his hair and twirling; Jameson could hear her whispering to him. Occasionally she pulled the head back, opening the cut across his neck seeming to create a two-way conversation between the two of them. Lowering her tone, Elena replied for him.

As the neck was opened, Jameson glimpsed the white of bone so he knew it was pretty fucking deep. Blood covered the table and a good portion of his uniform. She was a chip off the old block and had the drive and ability to do whatever asked of her. At a young age she had shown what she was capable of.

* * *

The night was upon them. Jameson had been personally dreading it and hoping that Elena would change her mind. He knew what happened on prom nights and he'd be damned if she was going to be another statistic and lose her virginity tonight. It was staggering how many people had sex for the first time on prom nights. What made that night so goddamn special was beyond his understanding.

He sat in his tattered green recliner nursing a beer, his sixth or seventh, waiting for his daughter and wife to come downstairs. It had been close to an hour already. How long could it possibly take to get ready? Not like he knew, but he figured it couldn't be all that difficult. Footsteps on the stairs brought his attention from the magazine he was reading as the pair descended.

The sparkling blue dress was beautiful and accented Elena's features. The beaming smile on her face spoke volumes and Jameson didn't want to ruin her night so he decided not to ask her if she wanted to go through with it still.

"So, what do you think?"

Elena's tone was one of pride, joy, and hope. His opinion and approval both meant the world to her.

"Beautiful. As always," Jameson answered with a forced smile.

A knock on the door announced her date and escort for the evening. Some football jock that, according to Elena, was very popular and well liked among all the students. Like he gave a shit about the kid and his ability to impress his friends. Jameson stood up and went to the door but was cut off by Elena.

"Please be nice daddy!"

Without answering, he opened the door expecting a tall, muscular jock. His expectations were way off. The boy was under six feet tall, and kind of scrawny with messy brown hair. Thankfully he wasn't wearing glasses or Jameson would have had a hard time not shutting the door in his face.

"Good evening Mr. Rifflet. It's nice to meet you." Followed by an extended hand which was expertly ignored.

"You play football?"

The question just slipped out and dripped of sarcasm. The boy's hand fell back to his side and his face reddened. Embarrassed.

"Dad," Elena groaned, nudging him in the side. "Brock is a receiver not a lineman. He's fast and has scored eight touchdowns this season."

Jameson nodded his head in mock approval.

"Eight huh. That's pretty good."

A small smile appeared on his face at the acknowledgment. Jameson moved to the side, allowing Eleanor to give her welcome and meet Elena's date. Settling back into his recliner, he tuned out the conversation that followed. He seemed harmless and the worry that had built up inside Jameson dissipated.

"What time will you be bringing my daughter home?"

"The prom ends at eleven so we should be back here no later than eleven forty-five sir."

"Eleven forty-five it is then."

The couple left giddy and excited to be heading to their senior prom. Jameson moved the curtain to the side and watched Brock open the passenger door for Elena. Good. Maybe he wasn't an asshole after all.

Eleanor resumed her knitting.

"Nice boy, don't you think?"

"Sure," Jameson replied, turning back to his magazine.

At eleven thirty the sound of a car could be heard pulling up to the driveway. Jameson didn't want to rush out and intrude on their "date", if that's what it was. Ten minutes went by and still Elena hadn't come in the front door. Pulling aside the curtain revealed an idling car with no motion from it. He could see two figures in the front seats, but their shadows weren't mingling so he wasn't concerned.

Five minutes later Elena burst through the front door like a freight train and bolted for the stairs.

"Whoa. Stop! Honey, what's going on?"

She froze at the first step and turned to him. Her eyes were puffy and red from crying and her make-up was smeared on her face. Blood covered the front of her dress and was on her hands.

"Oh my God. What the hell did he do to you?! I'll kill him!"

Her shaking body was the only response she gave. She let him lower her down to sit on the step and just mumbled incoherently.

"Stay here, I'll be right back," he said, then shouted upstairs, "Eleanor, get down here quick!"

He didn't wait for his wife to come down. Grabbing the baseball bat that was resting next to the front door, he marched out of the house, prepared to break Brock's legs, and eventually neck, muttering to himself the whole way.

"Son of a bitch... little fucker... hurt my daughter."

The rant stopped when he opened the driver's side door and the boy's body spilled out onto the ground. Blood and fluid leaked from the ruined mess where his eyes used to be, and a knife hilt protruded from his chest. This wasn't what he expected to see. Jameson was confused as he bent down and checked for a pulse. None.

The front door was still open, and he could see his wife sitting next to Elena, rocking her back and forth, asking her what had happened no doubt. Elena's gaze was fixed upon him. She wasn't in shock because Brock had hurt her but because she'd killed him. Jameson was speechless as he walked back into the house and looked down at his daughter. The words came out fast in an endless stream accompanied with tears.

"It wasn't my fault. I promise. When we pulled into the driveway, Brock kissed me, and I was getting ready to say goodnight, but he locked the car doors. He wouldn't let me out. He put his hand down my dress and... and... I thought he was going to rape me daddy!"

"Oh my God! Is he still out there Jameson? I've got a mind to teach him a thing or two."

Eleanor's face reddened in anger and disgust, not knowing that her daughter had singlehandedly taken care of the situation already. Jameson squatted down in front of them. He could tell that Elena thought he was mad at her, but he wasn't. He was impressed.

"It's okay sweetheart. You did the right thing. That son of a bitch had it coming to him. If you hadn't taken care of the situation, I would have."

Blood, and other liquid covered her fingers from where she'd gouged out his eyes. It didn't bother him. He hugged them both close to him. Eleanor's body stiffened in his embrace, and he knew it was because she'd finally seen the boy's body outside. He hugged them tighter. Under the tears, a smile appeared on Elena's face. She wasn't experiencing sadness or remorse at taking someone's life. The tears were because she thought for sure that her dad would blow his top when he saw what she'd done.

* * *

"I'm thrilled that you enjoyed the stew. Tell me again how wonderful I am…"

Elena's hand rested against his cheek. Hearing a cough from behind her she bolted upright and dropped her hand. No reprimand from her father who was looking at her with a gleam in his eyes. He walked over to her and put both hands on her cheeks, wiping a speck of blood away.

"You're my pride and joy sweetheart. Well done."

18

Viciously awakened by the agony radiating out from his shoulders, Warren had lost count of how many times he'd slipped in and out of consciousness. If he had to put a number to it, he'd guess in the neighborhood of six or seven times. The pain was constant now, and he was going to have to get used to it. It took some effort, but he forced it to the back of his mind. The throbbing eased slightly.

If he kept his movements to a minimum, the pain abated slightly but it was damn near impossible to keep still. Having your feet dangling four inches above the floor tended to do that. He was waiting for his collarbones to snap under the strain and the hooks to rip out of his flesh. It was a matter of when not if.

Sweat streamed down his body, partly from exertion but also from shock. His heart continued to pound, and his chest heaved with each breath.

The creaking of the door hinges caused him to raise his

head and squint through the sweat that dripped in his eyes. A woman was standing in the doorway. He waited to see if she would enter but she just stood there as still and silent as a statue.

Warren cleared his throat preparing to call out to her, when she moved. She glided forward slowly, head cocked to the side as if evaluating him, and stopped ten feet away from him. Hope sparked within his chest. This could be his chance at freedom. She didn't have the crazed look about her that the man from earlier had. What did he have to lose by trying to appeal to her humanity?

"Please help me," he pleaded in a soft voice.

She crept closer, tears filling her eyes. She reached up and gently placed her hand against his cheek, closing her eyes. A tear fell from her clenched eyes, soon followed by more. Desperate, Warren tried again to address the part of her that was obviously upset by what was being done to him.

"If you pull that chair over and place it under my feet, I think I can lift myself off of these hooks," he said, trying to keep his voice calm and neutral.

She gave no indication of having heard him. "Ma'am?"

19

There was no way to stop the images and memories from crashing upon her like a rogue tidal wave in her mind, overwhelming her thoughts. The man dangling from the hooks like a worm bore a striking resemblance to her father, the uniform only solidifying that image. Eleanor's breath had caught in her throat upon entering the storeroom as if her body had forgotten the simple act of breathing.

All the good times she'd shared with her father before he'd died at the young age of forty-five from a massive heart attack bubbled up to the surface. Trips, places, and events that she'd hidden away revealed themselves in their entirety and she let herself get carried away with the memories.

Her hand still resting against his cheek, Eleanor closed her eyes once more and let her father's persona take shape. Healthy, in remarkable shape for his age, he was an impressive man who carried himself as such. His only vice was that he smoked like a damned chimney from the age of fourteen which had weakened his heart over the years. A distinct and vivid memory formed and separated itself from the rest.

Her father dancing with her in the living room of their home when Eleanor was just ten years old. Even after working an exhausting twelve hour shift, he always made time for his sweet girl. He was her entire world.

The man's pleas for help caused the image of her father to shimmer and dissolve no matter how much she desired to keep it solid. When he suggested moving the chair over, Eleanor's eyes shot open, and she slapped him in the face to shut him up.

It worked.

Taking his hands in hers, she closed her eyes again and moved slowly from side to side, imagining herself dancing with her long dead father. Humming a tune helped transport her back in time to that night in the living room. Eleanor shoved the man's whimpering to the back of her mind and let her imagination take full control. Her father's laughter filled her ears and she could hear her mother encouraging them and singing along with the song. He swung her around the room like a ballerina, dipping her occasionally.

Something dropped onto her hand with a wet plop, rushing her back to the present. A drop of red glistened on her hand. The man's face contorted in pain, and he was grinding his teeth together to keep silent.

"You're never getting out of here. I'm so sorry," she whispered.

A creaking floorboard from the doorway and she instantly released his hands as if they'd burned her.

"Having fun, are we?"

20

Eleanor hurried from the room, head down, avoiding the amused gaze of her husband. Had her father not passed away so young, she probably would never have even dated Jameson, let alone marry him. Stepping through the doorway, she purged that line of thinking. Jameson walked over to Warren with a bounce in his step.

"I've got something for you, my friend. I got to thinking that you might be somewhat lonely in here and I want you to be as comfortable as possible. Considering the circumstances," Jameson said, touching the bloodied hooks. "Would you like some company? Might help to pass the time."

His stinking breath sickened Warren. Summoning the last reserves of strength he had, Warren swung his leg forward and brought it home between Jameson's legs. Crying out, Jameson dropped to the floor, shaking hands cradling his crotch. The satisfaction and joy Warren received was short lived.

"You... Fuck!" Jameson shouted, spit flying from his mouth. "You're going to regret that."

Wincing, Jameson regained his feet. Splotches of red appeared on his face as he retreated to a safe distance. Well out of Warren's reach.

"Gabe, go ahead and bring his friend in."

A scream of rage left Warren's throat raw as he watched the young man from the truck enter the room, Mac's body draped over his right shoulder. The gaping wound in his neck was a clear indication that he was dead. Gabe dropped him to the floor with a meaty thud.

Obscenities flew from Warren's mouth in no particular order, coupled with threats of pain and death towards the men that stood before him. Gabe flinched at the tirade and wouldn't look up at the enraged man rocking on the hooks, but Jameson simply drank it all in.

Mac's pale face stared up at the ceiling.

"Could you two please keep him quiet? Customers are beginning to pull into the parking lot," Eleanor's voice drifted from the direction of the kitchen.

Gabe picked up a bloody rag and roll of duct tape from his father's worktable as Jameson hefted a rusty wrench.

"My pleasure," Jameson said, moving closer to Warren. "We're just getting started here Officer Warren. Consider your partner lucky because you're going to beg for me to kill you before I'm done with you."

21

An elderly couple on vacation from South Carolina entered the restaurant, hoping to please their palates with a hot meal. After stopping for gas, the woman had hinted that she was hungry and spotted the sign for a place called Hunger Pains down the road a way. Eleanor greeted them at the door and escorted them to a table with a smile.

"Your waitress will be with you shortly," she said handing them each a menu.

A younger woman was wiping down a table across the restaurant but dropped the cloth upon seeing them get seated. With a skip in her step Elena approached, pad and pen in hand.

"Welcome to Hunger Pains. My name is Elena, and I will be serving you today. Can I get you started with a couple of drinks?"

"Two waters please," the old man responded respectfully.

"I'll be right back, and our special today is Jameson's Catch of the Day. If you have any questions about the menu, please don't hesitate to ask."

Elena strolled away to get their waters and winked at Gabe who was sitting on one of the counters in the kitchen. He looked through her and didn't bother with acknowledging her.

"What a lovely young lady. I'm so glad we stopped here Leonard."

Her husband put on his glasses to browse the menu.

"You do know how to pick out the best place to eat Grace. Their menu is definitely unique. I may have to splurge today and get some dessert. I wonder if we can get that for here or to go?"

* * *

"Out of my way. Move!"

He forced his way through the group of people who were chatting away, not caring if he was being rude or not. He even let a comment slide that otherwise would have had some consequences.

Helen, headset on, nodded to him as he approached. Whatever conversation she was in the middle of would have to wait.

"Any word yet?"

She shook her head in response while replying to whatever was being asked to her through the headset. His demeanor must have been easy to read because she quickly ended her call.

"Sorry Captain. It's been over two hours since we heard anything from Officer Warren, and we can't reach either one of them on the radio. The patrol unit has been dispatched."

Captain Forde paced back and forth in front of her desk,

clucking his tongue. Nervous habit that his wife hated.

"What was the location of their last transmission?"

"Give me one second," she replied, scanning the transcript on her desk. "A restaurant called Hunger Pains. I've never heard of the place."

He didn't recognize the name either and stormed off towards his office, stopping next to his secretary's desk.

"I want Ramirez, Jenkins, and Talbot in my office now. We're gonna find out what the fuck is going on. Let me know when the patrol unit gets there. And get me any information you can find on a restaurant called Hunger Pains."

22

Throughout the entire interview, he'd kept an eye out for some clue to how she'd felt about the information she was sharing. At the more colorful parts, Corder noticed Davis flinch slightly and even at one point mutter 'Dear God' under his breath. Typically, people being held on the charges she was facing would either display remorse hoping to gain sympathy or be completely shut off to any kind of emotion. Elena Rifflet's tone of voice came off as proud and her emotions hovered between elation and excitement while recalling events from that day. Particularly regarding Officer Mac's murder, which is the only one she claimed full responsibility for.

"You've only murdered one person? That's a terribly efficient way to end a person's life and you didn't even stop to think about the implications of your actions."

Displaying a half smile, she tilted her head at him. "I didn't say I only killed one person. You asked me to give more information that was currently unknown and that's what I did. Do I make you uncomfortable Detective Davis?"

Davis had stood up and was leaning against the wall, hand covering his mouth.

"Frankly, you disgust me."

She pouted at him before turning back to Detective Corder.

"All I want is to see the sun on occasion, and breath fresh air for a change. If you two can talk to the Warden about allowing me to go outside, with an armed escort of course, in the sunlight, I may consider going into more details about that day concerning what happened to Officer Warren. With him in critical condition in the ICU, you have no credible statements or information. Like it or not, I'm the best chance you have to sifting through all the theories and bull shit surrounding the case."

To Be Continued in Order Up...
Read on for a sneak peek.

23

Click HERE to purchase "Order Up", the third book in the ongoing series!!!